For Vicki, Jo and Stuart

Library of Congress Cataloging-in-Publication Data
Riches, Judith
Giraffes have more fun/by Judith Riches.—1st U.S. ed.   p.   cm.
Summary: Sally learns about giraffes in school and
decides to become one.
ISBN 0-688-11042-8 (trade)—ISBN 0-688-11043-6 (lib.)
[1. Giraffes—Fiction.] I. Title.
PZ7.R398394Gi 1992 [E]—dc20 91-21184 CIP AC

1 3 5 7 9 10 8 6 4 2

First U.S. Edition, 1992

Giraffes Have More Fun

by JUDITH RICHES

Tambourine Books · New York

This is a giraffe," said Mrs. Evans.

"You can see that he's a fine looking animal, with his patterned coat for hiding among the leaves. His long neck means he can easily grab the leaves from treetops with his strong tongue and with his long legs he can run faster than a horse."

"I'd love to be a giraffe," Sally thought. I bet it's more fun than being a little girl."

When Mom picked her up from school that afternoon, Sally couldn't wait to tell her all about giraffes.

"When I get home, I think I'll make myself a giraffe costume," she said.

She took out her paintbox,
and found the old toy horse
that she didn't play with
anymore.

"If I paint brown splotches on you, you'll make a very
good giraffe head," she told him. The toy horse didn't
disagree, and so she started painting.

Next, Sally painted some spots on an old sheet her mother gave her, and wrapped it around herself. Now she really did look like a giraffe.

"If I were a giraffe, I'd have an extra long stocking filled with presents at Christmas," she said.

"And with my long giraffe legs, I'd always win the high jump on Sports Day."

She especially liked that idea, because her own legs were rather short and she could never jump high enough to win.

Thinking about Sports Day and exercise made Sally feel hungry. Of course, now that she was a giraffe, she could reach the cookie jar without any trouble.

Mom walked into the kitchen. "One thing you forgot about giraffes is they're big, so it's easy to see them when they're being naughty," she said.

Sally thought it might
be a good time to play
outside. Dad had left the step-ladder in the
garden, so Sally climbed to the top for a giraffe's-
eye-view. She could see a lot from up there.
It would be very useful being tall, she thought.

She could rescue Mrs. Taylor's kitten the
next time it got stuck up in a tree, for instance.
Sally was having so much fun pretending
to be a giraffe that she forgot she was a
little girl.

So when Mom asked Sally to clean her bedroom and put away her paints, she said, "No, I'm a giraffe. Giraffes don't have to clean their bedrooms."

"In that case," said Mom, "you won't be able to have any ice cream. Giraffes don't eat ice cream. You'd better have some leaves instead.

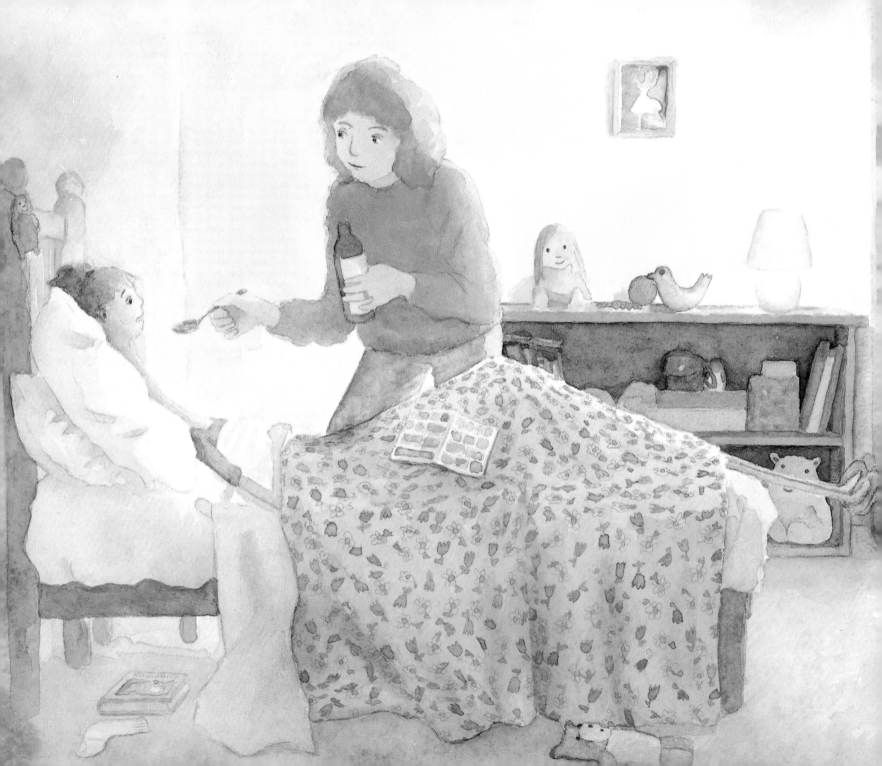

"And since giraffes have such long
necks, you'll have to swallow lots
of medicine the next time you get a
sore throat.

"And you can forget about your
new shoes, too, because giraffes don't
need to wear them.

"And soon you'll have grown into such a big giraffe that you won't be able to sleep in your own bed and have stories read to you. We'll have to put you out in the garden."

Sally tore off her giraffe outfit. Why, giraffes hardly had any fun at all!

"But I'm not a giraffe—I'm just a little girl!" she shouted, and she ran to Mom for a hug.

That night, after Sally was tucked in bed, Mom read her a story about elephants.

But later, when she was supposed to be asleep, she crept in to see her mother.

"Tell me more about elephants, Mom...."